The Adventurers - part

The episode of the tomb

By

Nathaniel Holland

Author's Note

'The Adventurers (part 1) - The episode of the tomb' is the first part the story, telling of the journey and the discoveries made by the man, the boy and the dog as they seek the source of the Nile, following a strange map.

This edition of 'The episode of the tomb' contains a sneek preview of part 2 of the story, 'The episode of the airship'.

'The Adventurers' is available in the Kindle Store and is also available in paperback, sold exclusively through Amazon.

'The Adventurers (part 1) - The episode of the tomb' was originally published under the author's name 'Alp Mortal'. Alp Mortal's children's stories are now published under the name 'Nathaniel Holland'.

If you want to find out more about this story please visit Nathaniel's blog at:

www.nathanielholland.weebly.com.

Or email Nathaniel at:

nathanielholland@hotmail.co.uk

The image used in the design of this cover was downloaded from Depositphotos, copyright 'goccedicolore'.

Nathaniel Holland

December 2013

Prelude

His mother died the second he was born; the cord hadn't even been cut when she issued her last breath. In the few minutes during which the shocking realisation dawned on everyone present, her spirit, her love, her beauty, her intellect and her soul were transmitted to the child, a beautiful healthy boy. He didn't cry; he just opened his eyes and waited for the rest to wail; as if their bums had been given a swift thwack.

He was always a knowing child, not unnervingly so, just quietly. In his own sweet-natured way, he knew and you knew he knew. It was difficult to lie to him, because he knew.

The father was a callous, selfish, self-centred and vain man, but a wealthy one. He placed the child with an older couple in the neighbourhood, paid them handsomely to look after the boy and not to bother him too much, just as long as appearances were maintained. He didn't want the smell of nappies pervading the house or piles of clothes and toys cluttering up his perfect home. The child was perfect; perfectly proportioned and stunningly beautiful. The mothers in the street couldn't take their eyes off of him; he just looked back with the clearest and bluest eyes from beneath feathery lashes under a growing mop of the blondest and curliest hair.

His surrogate mother whom we call Motty, his first word, cannot bear to cut his hair so she doesn't; it just grows and becomes thicker and curlier. His surrogate father whom we call Datty, his second word, worships his little boy and barely allows his feet to touch the ground because he always carries him and the boy has his arms around Datty's neck. Motty feeds him and changes him, bathes him and sings him to sleep, strokes his cheek and kisses his forehead, holds his perfect little hand and thanks her lucky stars because she can't have any children of her own.

He grows tall, strong and slim, perfect in limb and he runs and jumps and cartwheels; he laughs and shouts and Datty can hardly keep up, but he tries. Motty teaches him his letters and numbers and rhymes and songs; times tables and the names of the Kings and Queens of England and the stories from the Bible. Datty shows him how to tie his laces and his necktie, polish his shoes and how to grow things and look after the birds in the aviary and the fish in the pond.

Father believes the boy should have a dog and buys him a puppy, a Staffordshire terrier, velvety soft and well behaved; a brindle with white socks and a blaze on his chest. They are inseparable.

The boy grows and grows and is stronger and faster than any other child at school. He can catch the ball, bowl the ball, kick the ball, throw the ball, wield the bat and deliver a mighty thump but no-one challenges his position as ruler of the dominion.

He is never ill, has never taken to his bed with cold or fever, no stomach or head ache, no acne, no greasy skin or lanky hair, no odours or habits we don't like to mention; he's just a rudely healthy boy, always quiet, always right, always happy, always helpful, especially to Motty and Datty.

The dog is always at his side, looking up for the signs to run, to jump, to fetch, to carry, to lie down, to play dead, to sit up and to be quiet.

Motty and Datty are very proud for he has passed his tests. Father buys him a suit and good shoes, a necktie and three stiff collared shirts. Motty and Datty have very little but scrape together to buy him a watch. They retire from the village and go to the coast; he visits when he can. He never visits his father, but writes to him, editing the news.

His father is proud and pleased but sad too for he is alone. In the end he realises his mistake but it is too late. He leaves the boy his money and goes to Hell with one less piece of guilt. The boy, who is now a man, visits his grave, stands looking at the headstone for a minute and then turns away, never to see it again.

He visits Motty and Datty, giving them the money, silencing their protests with a kiss on each of their cheeks. He picks up his case and calls for the dog, which runs to his side. He opens the door and strolls out, smiling; turning briefly he waves and then he disappears round the corner.

The episode of the tomb

You will have to suspend belief and imagine a world without stupid rules like getting dogs their own passport; man and dog travel freely, often on ships and trains. The World is sepia tinted and uncluttered by fast food outlets and gaudy neon lights. It is full of harbours and stations, teeming with people with purpose; exotic scents and dislocated shouts above the roar of steam engines and the flapping of sails. Occasionally there is a car, more often the clop of a horse's hooves.

He and the dog wait at the edge of the south English port, waiting for the Captain of the ship to tell them to board. They are still but like wound springs; there is urgency and power in the set of their shoulders, man and dog alike. At last they are aboard and stowed below. Their cabin is fitted out in strange woods; the grain and knots drawing an entirely different atlas to the one he is used to. The boards creak which signals that the ship is moving, slipping away from the jetty and heading out into the sea. They rise and go above deck to watch the cliffs disappear and finally their view of the coast is extinguished; all around them nothing but the murky, foamy, blue-green sea. One looks down and one looks up and both smile in their way.

Their voyage is long, the winds are keen in the Bay and all hands are on deck to manage the sails. He does his part, takes his turn; gets cold, gets wet, gets sunburnt, gets tired, gets on with his fellow man, proves his worth, his metal and his salt. He learns fast and applies his knowledge quickly, deftly and he is liked, rewarded and will always be remembered as the Englishman with the dog.

They pass Gibraltar and head into the Mediterranean

Sea.

They meander from port to port, buying and selling; he adds to his capital shrewdly. He changes his clothes, sheds the suit and barters with it in exchange for breeches, strong boots, linen shirts and a good leather belt. He trades the case for saddle bags and buys a gun. He haggles for maps and a knife with a sharp blade. His smile weakens any resistance. His shipmates insist that he has a tattoo; he sits bravely in the chair as the Chinaman prepares the needle and the ink. He's chosen a rose wrapped around an anchor. He grits his teeth and slugs at the bottle, dulling the pain.

The rose is for his country and the anchor for his friends.

It's done, they celebrate and he laughs at his mock bravery, it hurt like Hell he says. They stagger back drunk and the dog is unimpressed that his reverie is disturbed and grunts in disapproval. He cuffs the dog, which bites him, to remind him that they are brothers. The man falls into his bed. The morning is still, quiet and bright. The man awakes, eyes the dog and says he is sorry. The dog licks his hand and then his face. The bite leaves a scar, the first of many.

They dock at Alexandria; the air is heavy, laden with spice and the noise of trade. This is where they part, man and dog from the crew. They hug and laugh and shout and cry and hug once more. Gifts are given; there's gold from the Captain, sadder than most to lose a man worth his salt; there's silver from some and good advice from all. He's packed and ready.

The dog pads at his side, looking around for danger and raising a lip if anyone gets too close. The man stops to ask the way. A lad of ten years espies them and smiles shyly at the dog. The dog grunts and the boy is invited to pat his head and tickle his ears.

"Where are you from lad?"

"Across the ocean," says the boy with a broad gesture, stabbing vaguely west.

"Do you want to go home?"

"I want to be free and have adventures like the boys I read about in the books on my master's shelf."

"Can you read?" asks the man a little dubiously.

"A little …"

"What else?"

"I can cook, mend and clean boots, whet a knife and light a fire …"

"Commendable skills. Where is your Master?"

"In the big house; he is like you …"

"Take me to him."

The men meet, sit and drink tea, smoke hash and talk. Gold is exchanged, though not much. The Master shouts and the boy comes running, his pack on his back.

The boy is slim and brown with fuzzy black hair. His body is like gnarled old witch-hazel twigs joined with gummed twine. He is quick. He has linen pants and a linen shirt. His feet are bare and calloused; his hands are strong and calloused. He has all his teeth, pearly white and a ring of gold in each ear; a gift from his mother as she died giving birth. A pact is made, silently.

"Where are we going?" asks the boy.

"South, along the river to the distant mountains."

"On foot?"

"By horse."

They buy a horse and camping gear, sturdy, both. The dog eyes the horse and the horse eyes the dog; they reach an understanding.

They leave the city and head south. They halt. They camp and light the fire. The boy cooks squash in a rich sauce with bread. The night is cold. The stars wheel above their heads.

The moon rises. The boy is asleep, curled up like a cat against the belly of the dog which in turn is curled up against the belly of the horse. The man retires. He is woken by steaming tea and hot water in a bowl to wash his face.

"No, my lad; you need not wait on me but the tea is welcome."

The man rises and steps out to the chill of the dawn. He strips off and runs to the river, plunging in.

"Come on lad; wash away the dust."

The boy is reluctant but finally sheds his clothes. He runs in too but not before the man has seen the scars on his back, on his legs and on his arms.

"You do not need to tell me who or why; I can guess. Have no fear. I will never hurt you."

They splash and dive and race.

"Grab hold of my neck and take a deep breath," says the man.

They dive; the man kicks strongly and they descend. The water is not very deep here near the bank and after a few powerful strokes they have reached the bottom. The man turns but as he does he sees something shiny in the murky gloom. Reaching out a hand, he grabs the thing and then bounces to propel them to the surface. They break through, laughing.

They lie on the bank to dry in the early morning sun.

The man examines the strange, shiny thing. It is an

amulet; a flat disc with strange markings. There is a hole in the centre of the disc. He threads it on a thong and places it around the boy's neck. The boy is pleased and tells him it is a lucky charm; their journey will be blessed by the Gods.

"If our way is straight and our feet tread surely, if we have water and food and the horse does not fall lame then I shall say we are lucky enough."

They pack and start off, heading south. Veering inland by a mile or two at times to find a firmer path, they make good time, rest under the blazing midday sun and travel later in the day when it is cooler. The horse carries the gear and they walk mostly. The dog runs back and forth, chasing imaginary scents, looking earnestly into every hole. He is happy nonetheless. The horse plods on slowly at the walking pace; happy too. The bundle is light compared to some he has carried and there is food and water.

They make camp. Twenty-five miles they have covered and the lush green belt beside the river is welcome after a dusty day. They bathe and the boy lights the fire and cooks fish with a little rice. The man brews tea and adds some grog so they are warmer against the chill night.

The dog curls up against the belly of the boy, the boy the man, the man the horse; each with a quarter eye and a quarter ear open. Snakes, frogs and other beasts with razor sharp teeth and thick leathery hides steer a wide berth of this strange multi-legged, multi-armed and multi-headed beast which snores in four octaves. The tent fared less well and the remains of the fish were gone by morning.

They continue their journey, resting frequently.

"Where are you from?" asks the boy.

"An island in the English Channel..."

"Is it covered with palms and fringed by sand?"

"It has many fine beaches and there are a few palms but mostly it is covered by grass and there are sheep ..."

"Sheep?"

"Like goats but smaller, shorter necked, woolly coated ..."

"Woolly?"

"Their hair is like your hair ..."

"How strange they must be!" the boy laughs.

"Where are you from boy?"

"The Caribbean, the island of Saint Lucia ..."

"I don't know of this place. I have never crossed the ocean but if I can I shall take you home one day ..."

"My Mother is dead and my Father is dead; there is no-one there. Why should I want to go back?"

"To buy a plantation and grow coffee and tobacco and cotton with which to make your fortune."

"I have no money ..."

"Yet!"

"Why are we going South?"

"To have an adventure and maybe find diamonds or gold ..."

They walk and ask questions of each other. The boy never tires of hearing about the man's island the man never tires of hearing about the boy's, albeit both remember them very fondly and maybe myth has overtaken fact in some parts. We are all guilty of that when we miss our home.

"We need a boat then we should get to the South much faster," said the boy as they ate that night beneath a moonless sky with stars so bright they cast shadows.

"Maybe we would, but what about the cataracts? We should have to abandon the boat and the horse cannot ride in the boat with us, so then what should we do? I prefer to travel with my horse, but I agree a boat would be much quicker. We shall see what we find in Cairo ..."

"We must cross the river then if we are going to the city. We are on the west bank and Cairo is on the east; but the Pyramids and the Sphinx are on our side ..."

"You know much ..."

"I read my master's books and he had a map."

"We shall see. I would like to see the Pyramids and the Sphinx. Whether we abandon the horse and obtain ourselves a boat, I cannot yet say. I have a feeling that we will have many difficult choices ahead of us ..."

They walk on. Sometimes the man puts the boy in the saddle and he sleeps; the man never seems to tire on the road, although he sleeps soundly every night. The dog runs backwards and forwards, busy in his own little World. Staffordshire's are most happy when their noses are a hair's breadth above the ground and fully employed!

"How old is the dog?" asks the boy.

"He is nineteen years ..."

"That is very old. How is it that he scampers like a puppy ..."

"He is a Staffordshire. The very best of his kind will live to be twenty-seven; even then I am sure he will be the same. They are indomitable, imperishable and faithful to their last breath. He would never allow a thing to harm you or me; it is his nature; but he can be strict and has bitten me for being a fool ..."

They stop to rest during the fiercest part of the day but even their daily habit has not stopped the Sun from tanning the man to the colour of mahogany. He is nearly as dark as the boy.

The man thanked his foresight in changing his suit for breeches and boots but his feet are hot and the boots often full of sand. The villagers they pass wear sandals; merely soles of leather with a strap to keep them on their feet. He barters for a pair. The villager is mightily pleased with the boots; although his feet are so weathered they looked like a pair of well-worn but cherished boots, perhaps the kudos of owning such a pair was greater than their utility.

The villagers wear either a pair of linen trousers which do not extend lower than the calf or a kaftan. The man thought the linen pants a good deal more to his liking and he bartered for a pair. Most of the village men wear no shirt but the man keeps his linen shirts and the broad brimmed hat.

Motty had never cut his hair as a boy and neither has he. It has grown thick and curly, the colour of ripe corn; it is long and he ties it back, like the sailors he had worked alongside. He keeps his chin shaved close. The boy is in awe as he watches him scrape the sharpest blade across his face without a nick or a cut.

Both had bathed and were drying in the early sun. The dog sat a little way off, watching the water nervously and with good reason; it swirled in eddies and shadows played beneath its surface. With a quick and powerful flick of its mighty tail a Nile crocodile lunged up and out of the water, less than ten feet from the bathers who were taken unaware. The dog barked sharply and the man turned to see the fearful jaws of the crocodile turn and open; powerful shoulders manoeuvring the beast for the two or three strides that would suffice for it to reach him.

Fortunately the boy was the other side of him and not in imminent danger. He had turned and had crawled away as soon as the dog barked, remembering the words of the man about the dog's instinct to protect them; he never barked unless danger was present.

Even a Staffordshire as fearless as this one is no match for a fifteen foot crocodile whose hide is as think as riveted plate with teeth three inches long and razor sharp.

The huge beast had turned and was taking its first step. The man had no chance to get up and run; this fact probably saved him. Lying as he was the creature had less to aim for and no purchase and so it merely pushed him like a log. The force of that was enough to break the man's ribs. He rolled once so that he was lying on his front. The brute advanced again and as it did the man pushed himself up and landed on top of the beast which immediately raised its head and thrashed its tail. Raising its head was its first and only mistake for the dog lunged this time and with teeth that can crush bone, ripped out the throat of the crocodile while the man wrestled with its head.

The beast turned and rolled with the man back into the water, thrashing and spewing bright red blood. For what seemed like hours but in truth was maybe ten seconds, both man and crocodile were submerged, the water boiling, turning a darker shade of crimson all the while. In a final death throe the crocodile threw off the man who scrambled out of the water as the rest of the pack smelling the spilled blood, fell upon their brother and began to rip him to shreds.

The man stumbled further from the edge and then he fell down, clutching his side, screaming out in pain. The dog was instantly at his side, standing defensively; his muzzle stained red. The boy sat by the camp petrified and incapable of movement or speech, even when a few of the villagers arrived upon hearing the commotion. Two of the men tended to the man and carried him to the village, shouting ahead for water to be boiled. One of the women, upon seeing the boy, picked him up like a bundle of sticks and, pressing him firmly to her body as she carried him, she ran to the stockade.

Three days the man lay with fever raging, burning like the scorching sun outside whilst the boy, who never left his side, bathed his face with cool water. The dog sat on one side of his bed and the boy on the other. The horse, spooked by the attack had been found and brought back; he stood by the door to the hut, head hung low.

On the morning of the fourth day the fever broke and the man opened his eyes. He moved slightly and pain zigzagged across his face but he smiled when he saw the boy and the dog. The horse snickered outside; the family was reunited. Over the course of the next few days the man grew stronger and slept more peaceably, the boy and the dog his constant guardians, rarely taking their eyes from his chest as it rose and fell more strongly.

His side was bruised from under his arm to the top of his leg, a lurid mixture of purple, black and red. Astoundingly, the skin remained unbroken but three ribs were broken and he was bound with strips of linen holding a paste of herbs to his side which drew the bruising and eased the pain. Within a week of the attack he was walking; leaning on the boy with one hand and the saddle of the horse with the other, making circuits of the village to regain his strength.

The dog followed on his heels.

The boy was quiet and the man was concerned that the shock had been too much but his reasoning was off the mark.

"What is wrong lad?"

The boy bowed his head and wouldn't catch his eye.

"Tell me; I am going to be fine. There is no reason to be concerned anymore …"

"I was afraid and couldn't move to help you. I am ashamed of my weakness and ..."

The boy shook as sobs broke through the crust of his emotions which had set over the last week; a mixture of love, fear and shame.

The man, stunned by the confession, turned and knelt beside the boy; enveloping him in his arms he pulled the youngster to himself. The boy threw his arms around the man's neck and buried his face in his hair, crying. For a long time, well after the sobs had subsided, they held each other and said nothing. They broke their embrace and the man got up, wincing in pain but determined not to show a trace of it. The dog padded over and licked the boy's tear stained face and it tickled which made him laugh.

The tension and the weight of the emotion were dispelled.

After another week the man was strong enough to leave. He aided the villagers to repair a roof and mended a door or two, leaving a coin for the medicine.

Packed with fresh supplies, including dried crocodile meat, they left the village and turned south.

"How far are we from Cairo?" asked the boy.

"I'd say a hundred miles by my reckoning; a four or five day trek at our normal pace. I am beginning to think the boat would be better and swifter. We cannot take the rest of our lives to reach the mountains."

"We should have to leave the horse."

"Most likely you are right as I do not see how we can carry the horse in one of these small boats but a larger boat will need a crew ..."

"We could board a larger boat, one of the barges; they carry horses. I've seen them ..."

"Perhaps; as you rightly say, if we abandon the horse and take a small boat we would have to abandon it at the cataract and then we should have neither."

"A smaller boat could be carried around the cataract," replied the boy.

"Let us think again and decide once we reach Cairo. There we will either sell the horse and buy a small boat light enough to perhaps carry around the cataract or we will take the barge to Swenet and then ride."

The four or five days that it took to reach the city were uneventful; at least, they were not attacked by wild beasts!

Since the incident with the crocodile there was more of a sense of brotherhood between them. The near loss of the man had shaken them all, not least the man himself, realising that the motley band of horse, dog and boy were the nearest thing he probably had to family now.

"I think I can see the Pyramids in the distance," said the man.

"Then we are a day from the Giza plateau."

"Have you been there before?" asked the man.

"It is where I was sold to the master. I do not clearly recall how I got there."

"We will stay for a day or two and make our plan."

As they travelled, the Pyramids came into view and loomed large. Neither the boy nor the man had seen anything as big and the Sphinx left them both speechless; each looked at the other with eyes wide in wonder. They arrived late in the afternoon and camped on the plateau, a distance of a mile or two from the cluster of pharaohs' tombs. The sun set quickly and the moon rose on its tail.

They ate the remains of the dried meat and a little bread with some figs and dates and made the tea. It was cold and they wrapped themselves tightly in their blankets, curling up against the horse. The dog eyed every shadow warily but later, as the moon began to sink, lay down by their feet, Sphinx-like; recumbent but ever watchful.

Dawn broke and the sun warmed them quickly and the shimmer of the heat from the surface of the sand made the city on the opposite bank appear to float above the surface of the Nile.

They walked around the base of the largest Pyramid, avoiding the flocks of chattering guides which swarmed like flies. The boy shouted in their own tongue and they desisted.

"I never saw such a thing or its equal yet in my life and I wonder if I ever will," was all the man could say.

They wandered for an hour or two, visiting the Sphinx and stopping to drink a little water and to eat the remaining crust of bread in their bag.

"It is past noon; we shall have to travel swiftly to reach the city by sunset. The horse will have to carry us both," declared the man.

They rode due east and turned slightly north to hit the road to the city of Cairo. They reached the city just before sunset and found lodgings with livery for the horse. That night they ate well and slept in beds.

Light glinted off the amulet around the boy's neck and the man was determined to decipher the hieroglyphs before they ventured much farther.

The following day they busied themselves with plans and supplies. A final decision had to be made. They wished to travel independently and that ruled out the barge which was crowded and expensive, catering for increasing numbers of tourists, many of them English and French. The larger boats would indeed carry the horse but they needed a crew and it definitely would only carry them to Swenet where they would need to trek around the cataract but they would have the horse, However, the hire of the boat and the crew was more than ten times the cost of a smaller boat, which they could fund from the sale of the horse.

After much deliberation they sold the horse and bought a small boat, a sturdy and sound vessel, the man being well acquainted with boats after his journey south from England.

Their activity drew a crowd, mainly of boys the same age as the lad. None were brave enough to venture too close; the dog looked fearsome, still baring traces of the red blood of their vanquished foe.

Among the crowd were a few men, typical Egyptians of the merchant class and an older man, dressed plainly, who eyed the boy's amulet. He gestured to the man and waved for him to move closer, mumbling a few words which no one else could hear. The man strode over to him and they spoke a few words, turned and left together to enter a small house a little distance from the quay side.

The lad called a few of the boys over and showed them how to greet the dog who revelled in the attention, increasing the capital of the boy amongst his peers.

The man returned, his face a mask of deep concentration.

"We must leave now," was all he said.

They cast off and drifted into the middle of the river, gaining speed as the sail picked up the hot breath of the desert and within minutes the city was disappearing behind them.

"What did he say; the old man?" asked the boy.

"He wanted to ask me about the amulet and when I described the markings he told me that they mean

'PROTECTOR' in my tongue. He was keen to know where we found it and when I told him, he was more than curious to see it but I had an inkling his motives were not as honest as he would have me believe."

"I have seen a picture of the amulet in a book at my master's house. In the picture it is worn by a young priest and rays of light shine out from the centre …"

"Are you sure it was the same?"

"Yes, I'm sure."

"The old man was keen to see it and I'll wager he has seen the picture too," the man mused.

"It didn't protect *you*," said the boy.

"Well, I'm alive and so are you; perhaps its power is weak with age or neglect or maybe it doesn't work over a distance."

"Perhaps it is I who is weak …"

"That is not true and I don't want to hear you say it. My bravery nearly cost me my life and that was stupid."

"What shall we do with it now?" asked the lad.

"Nothing; wear it under your shirt. Doubtless its secret will be revealed at the proper time. Now take the rudder and steer a path straight; we need to put some distance between ourselves and the city; I shall feel better when the city is an hour or two behind us."

They sailed, steady and sure in the centre of the river, watching huts and temples and villagers fishing slip by. The man stretched out on the bunk in the small cabin, an arm over his eyes to capture an hour's repose. The boy steered their course true and the dog lounged on the deck, quite at home after his own experience of the journey from England. Before sunset they found an inlet and moored the boat to light a fire on the shore and cook their meat; goat kid, stewed with a few vegetables and eaten with a little rice.

Sailing was swifter and less tiring. The boat was easy to handle and the country on either side seemed to be moving past them as they sat still in the centre of the broad and noble Nile. There was time for teaching, storytelling and bits of mending and fishing. The lad was adept and they never felt hungry, although the dog was itching for the chase.

At villages along their way they bartered for bread and rice and a little meat with the stuff they had bought in the market. The boy was better at brokering than the man but he insisted that the dog stay at the boy's side and the amulet remain hidden; although he never suggested that the boy remove it, for he believed it did protect him and the stasis that the boy had taken to be paralysing fear was something else far more powerful which he did not yet understand.

One thing was evident; the longer the boy wore the amulet the brighter it became and the markings were easier to see. At first it seemed as though they were just scratched onto the surface but in fact they were deep and skilfully applied. At the centre of the disk was a hole but upon examination it looked as if it should have held something; maybe a gem. It definitely had the look of a jewel's setting.

If it were evident that the amulet was reacting to the boy then it was just as true that the boy was reacting to it. He had grown, not just in height and girth but his hair was lustrous and his eyes were brighter, taking on the hue of an earthy but vivid ochre.

The boy and the man slept in the cabin, which in reality was a tented area around the mast. Towards dawn the boy started mumbling and the noise woke the man. The boy's words were incomprehensible; not gibberish but of a different language and he was moving, thrusting out his arms. His movements became more violent and he had begun to scream. The man shook him to wake him from the nightmare.

"Lad; wake up!"

The boy fell silent. After a minute or two he opened his eyes.

"What was it lad; a bad dream?"

"I saw a vision; it was so real. I was standing in a temple, wearing strange clothes and the amulet was around my neck. Light shone out from its centre and the crowd was chanting. I felt a force boiling up and out from my heart which created the light which in turn shone out from the amulet, bathing the temple and the crowd in a reddish light ..."

"What happened?"

"I couldn't see. A mist descended over my eyes and I woke up."

"Lie quietly for a while."

The boy lay on his back with the amulet nestled between the hardening muscles of his breast, exactly in the centre of his chest. It was brighter and the markings were deeper and darker than the day before. The rest of the day passed without incident and the lad busied himself with a hundred chores; although mostly he sat and fished. They drew into the shore for the evening and to let the dog off to run. That night the sky was moonless and the only light came from the fire. Just before the pair retired, the boy clutched his breast, screaming out that the amulet was burning him.

The man jumped over to him and pulled his hand away. The amulet was indeed hot and pressed against his skin, almost as if it was burrowing into the flesh. He pulled it away, burning his fingers as he yanked the chord which held it. The amulet came free and he threw it onto the ground. Immediately it dimmed and grew cool.

The burning disk had left a mark on the boy's chest. The markings on the disc had cut right through the metal and had begun to incise the flesh, cauterising the edge of the wound as it sank deeper. A perfect facsimile of the markings, etched in red, was left behind in his coffee-caramel skin.

The man picked up the amulet and discovered that it looked no different to the day he had found it. The brightness and the depth of the markings had gone; it was dull and the markings mere scratches on the surface.

"It looks like its job has been accomplished, if that was its purpose; to mark you out. How do you feel now?"

"I don't know the words; both cool and hot. There is a reed singing in my chest, vibrating in the wind."

The man eyed him closely. The ochre hue of his eyes was less vivid but still bright and his hair still a mass of black lustrous coils.

"If you can, lie down in the cabin and try to rest."

"What do you think it means?"

"I cannot be sure but if the amulet holds an ancient power and that power can alter you, as we have seen it do already, then it must be treated with more respect ... and we need to know more before we can decide what to do. The old man said the markings meant 'PROTECTOR' so I am less concerned but still; it has scarred you."

"Will you sell me now?" asked the lad in a pitiful voice.

The man looked at him, his throat clamped with a surge of emotion, his eyes welling with tears. He took hold of the boy and pressed him close to his chest.

"No, never, you are my son..."

The boy returned the embrace and squeezed hard. The man could feel the heat from the scar on the lad's chest and wondered what transformation had occurred and what might have happened if he had not plucked the amulet off when he had. They placed the amulet in a small cloth bag and put it in the wooden box which held the man's gun and ammunition; a box he kept locked.

The next few days were silent. The air was laden and the sky was the colour of lead. There was no wind. The boat drifted on currents; however, progress was slow and without some sail to assist with the manoeuvres there was a constant risk of grounding in the shallows.

They moored the boat.

Finally a storm broke and the wind and rain were let loose in a fearful maelstrom. Cowering on the bank with the boat pulled out as far as they could manage, the man and the boy huddled together to wait out the storm. The dog hated the thunder and crawled between them, shaking and shivering, his ears pressed back and his tail wedged firmly between his legs.

The storm raged all day and all night for three days; its death throes the most violent of its phases. Lightening pierced the ground all around them and the river boiled ceaselessly. After three days, the clouds began to break and the wind dropped. The bedraggled trio peered out from behind the boat and cast off their blankets.

A ray of sun, liberated from the leaden skies of only moments earlier speared its way through and picked out the boy as he stood on the bank. The shaft of light, no wider than a finger, hit him dead in the centre of the scar on his chest. He collapsed without a sound.

The dog barked and ran to his side, whimpering, pawing him but the boy's body was lifeless. The man sank to his knees at the boy's side and pushed his hair away from his face which was serene, a smile on his lips.

Fearing the worst, he put his ear to the boy's chest which although still hot, the man could make out the faint beating within. The boy's breath was so shallow the man could barely feel it on his cheek. He lifted him gently and placed him on the bunk in the boat.

He sat as his side with the dog and waited.

They remained at his side for two days. The man was tired to his core, the emotions draining him of every ounce of his strength.

The boy stirred but didn't wake up. The man bathed him for his skin was searing hot; hottest most at the centre of the scar where the ray of light had entered his body.

Then the change began.

A fine tracery of lines started to appear, emanating from the centre of the scar. The lines, some the thickness of only a hair began to draw a map in remarkable and intricate detail. The lines were mostly red and they stood out against the boy's dark coffee-caramel skin. Some of the lines would end at strange shapes, perhaps the footprint of a temple whilst others would weave their way to cities and towns known to the man from his map, against which he compared the map being drawn on the boy's body. Some of the lines coincided perfectly; others did not appear on his copy and some shown on his map did not show on the boy's skin.

He concluded that the map being drawn in front of his very eyes was a map of the country from a much earlier time. Since then the old roads had disappeared beneath the sands. The outlines of the temples were much sharper and more detailed. He saw Pyramids at Giza of which no trace could now be seen.

The map extended all over the lad's body; his arms and legs, his torso, stomach and back, but not on his face.

The scar's centre was not, as he had assumed, Cairo; no, that was on the back of his left hand, the fingers of which were covered in the network of waterways towards Alexandria; so the map could be orientated and if his hand was Cairo then his arm was much of the country along the Nile, as far as the first cataract, at Swenet.

The centre of the scar, also the centre of the map, was clearly in the middle of the Nubian Desert.

When the map was finished the boy's eyes opened and he gasped, the air rasping in his throat. The man held a cup to his lips and the boy drank deeply.

"Lad, speak!"

"I have taken the most marvellous journey throughout the country and beyond the borders of most maps. There are hidden temples and cities buried beneath the sands, holding riches enough to buy the World ..."

"Easy boy, take your time; the storm has abated. It has been nearly three days since the sun pierced you and you fell. How is your chest; is it still hot?"

The boy touched the scar and found it to be cool, perhaps a little cooler than the rest of his skin. A patch on his left arm, near the crease of his elbow was red and hot.

"This is where we are. I can sense it and there is a connection."

"Astounding!" was the only word the man could summon.

"Should we follow the map to the centre in the desert? Something inside me seems desperate to go that way."

"We shall see. I would like to follow one of the lines to a temple which is not shown on the map I have; to see if there is any sign. If this map is true then the temple will be there but hidden and if what you sense can be relied upon, the red hot patch will move to that place with us."

"I am afraid," said the boy.

"Don't be lad; I and the dog will look after you."

"Which of the lines shall we follow?"

"A little further south there is a line which branches away from the river and ends due west at a temple maybe five miles from the river's bank. It is not marked on my map."

A remarkable fact remained un-remarked upon. As the map was drawn by the forces of the amulet and the sun, all of the boy's scars from the whippings he had endured at the hand of his cruel master, had been erased.

They dragged the boat back into the water and set the sail. The breeze picked up and soon they were slipping past the country, feeling stronger and surer. Their purpose was still vague but adventure to find diamonds and gold was certainly no less promising after the events of the last three days; perhaps even more likely if the boy's vision was true.

After a day on the water and a night on the bank and another day on the water they found the likely spot where the path led to the temple. If they had scanned the terrain very slowly and carefully, particularly at dusk, they would have just been able to make out a path, at least the echo of a path.

They camped, determined to follow the path in the morning of the new day ahead. They camped and ate heartily, the boy's appetite having returned.

They drew up the boat, hiding it under the fronds of palms and then set off on the hike of five miles; first through the lush margin of the river and then the land giving way to desert. The man had a compass and they kept to a dead straight path, due west. The terrain was easier to traverse than they thought, adding more weight to the idea that the ancient path was indeed beneath their feet. Two hours later they stopped. Ahead, there was a slight depression in the sand, barely discernible and a few rocks littered about but nothing else.

They walked all over the bowl, turning over the rocks and kicking at the sand.

"Is your arm hot?"

"Yes, very hot, we must be at the right place; the heat is exactly over the drawing of the temple."

"Then it must be beneath us ..."

The man had barely uttered the words when the earth opened up and he disappeared, shouting all the while. After a minute his voice could be heard again.

"Boy, be careful! The drop isn't long; the roof has collapsed."

The boy and the dog peered over the side of the hole into a sunken chamber. The man was standing and with his arms outstretched he could just reach the edge. In the dim light an opening was visible on one side of the chamber, leading down into the pitch black.

"What should I do?" asked the boy

"Jump down; I will catch you!"

The boy jumped and the man caught him, placing him squarely on his feet. The dog whined above their heads and he too jumped, landing in an untidy heap, letting out a squeal, more of embarrassment than actual pain.

They surveyed the chamber which was roughly square. The stone roof had collapsed under the weight of the man. The air was stale but freshening now that the chamber was open.

"Are you ready for the adventure that I promised you?" asked the man.

The lad just grinned and the dog was already at the opening.

"How shall we see?"

"There are fire brands in the wall sockets. Let's hope they will light."

They did, despite their age. They were dry and crackled but cast out sufficient light to see beyond the opening to the corridor. They stepped through, the dog just ahead and the boy firmly grasping the man's hand. The tunnel was dry and the floor was sandy and it proceeded for thirty paces until it opened into a larger room.

The room was empty but it had an opening to the left. They stepped forward, turned and passed through it into another tunnel; this time of sixty paces and the angle of which made for a steep incline. At the bottom of the incline they entered another room but this time a wondrous sight welcomed them. The walls were brightly painted in scenes from the history of some great Pharaoh. The room held a quantity of great stone jars, wooden boxes bound in copper and heavy granite sarcophagi.

Beyond the limit of the light they just could just see a doorway, angled so that the passage beyond was not visible. They went through and the passage turned tightly and quickly several times before it opened out, descending some one hundred paces at a steady incline. At the bottom, the passage turned several more times before opening into a small chamber completely devoid of paintings on the walls or objects save for the sarcophagus which was placed in the centre of the room.

"The Pharaoh's tomb," said the man quietly, more to himself than to his companions, "I do not think we should disturb the tomb. They say it brings bad luck, even death to the trespassers. Let us return to the chamber above."

They ascended the incline and re-entered the room which held the jars, the boxes and the smaller sarcophagi.

"The Pharaoh's treasure?" asked the boy.

"Undoubtedly; and if the legends are true then the treasure here will be rich but ... I am dissuaded from looting it, although the roof collapse above will mean that the treasure will not remain undisturbed for long. Well; that is the choice of any looters and they will have to take their chances with the curse."

A small box sat near one of the jars, a box made of ebony and inlaid with ivory pieces. The markings were identical to the markings on the amulet.

The boy had picked it up.

"Let me take that boy, at least until we are back outside. I fear what it may hold."

The lad handed it over and they ascended the passageway to the empty room, making their way back to the first room which was open to the sky.

"How will we escape? The edge looks too far and it may give way."

"If I can jump high enough I can reach the edge and pull myself out, then I shall reach in for you and haul you out."

"What of the dog?"

"I see in hindsight it would have been better to have prevented him from following us down but he is curious, more like a cat than a dog; it will be his undoing!"

"There is rope aplenty in the boat but I did not bring any. I noticed a coil in the chamber below which may serve to make a cradle for you and he, with which I can safely haul you up. Stay here whilst I fetch it."

The man returned two minutes later with the coil of

rope which he slung over his back and with two or three attempts he had gained the edge of the roof opening and had hauled himself out. Weeks hauling ropes and sails had prepared him for the task.

He fashioned a basic cradle, more of a noose than a cradle and let it down to the boy.

"Put you head and arms through and fasten it under your arms. Tell me when you are ready and I will pull."

The boy did as he was bidden and signalled to the man to pull him up. The rope creaked but did not give way and slowly, the man hoisted the boy until he was able to reach out and grab the edge for himself, swinging his leg to the side and gaining sufficient purchase to propel himself up and forward and out on to the sand.

"Go to the edge lad, out of this bowl; the roof may give again."

The man let the rope down again and the dog stepped in to the noose. The man pulled to tighten the rope around his body and then he hauled him up with very little effort, although the dog was yelping as the rope bit cruelly into his flesh.

Finally they were out and they moved to the side of the depression.

"Well, that was more adventure than I bargained for but it proved that the map is accurate and now we have the box which bears the same strange inscription. I barely dare to think what it might hold."

The boy took the wooden box from the man's hand and eased off the lid which was tight.

It contained some wadding which the boy removed to reveal another box. He pulled it out. It was perfectly square, a cube made of wood; the joints were invisible. On one side there was a depression, the precise thickness and diameter of the amulet; or so they judged by looking at the scar on the boy's chest.

"The amulet is on board the boat and that is where we should head. I am sorry that we cannot repair the roof of the tomb and let the King and his treasury rest in peace. Perhaps the prize will remain unfound for a while longer."

They returned to the boat. It would only be in the morning when they would discover that the line of the map leading from the bank of the river five miles due west had disappeared from the boy's skin. Unbeknown to man and boy, anyone walking in the area of the tomb now would see a slight depression and nothing more than undisturbed sand and a few rocks.

Back at the boat they recovered the amulet and pressed it into the depression on the side of the box. It fitted snugly. Nothing happened.

Tired and hungry they left the box and the amulet in the cabin and ventured for a swim before lighting the fire and cooking some fish. The dog lounged at their feet licking his sides which were red; scraped sore from the rope which was now neatly stowed in the boat. In the morning they found the rope had disintegrated and only dust remained, forming a ring on the planks of the deck.

"What is our plan?" asked the boy.

"I am torn between two goals," said the man, adding, "I dearly wish to follow the map to the centre of the desert but that journey is hundreds of miles and not only do we have no horse but we should soon have to leave the boat behind. I also wish to follow the river south to the mountains as I originally intended and in that direction we will fare better if we can carry the boat around the cataract ..."

"What is drawn on the map at the end of the river? I cannot see as it is on my back."

Indeed the map did trace the length of the river; up the boy's arm and across and down his spine to its base where the elaborate footprint of a temple was drawn. It looked like an angry mouth from which the river's water spewed. The man described it to him.

"I should go there if the choice were mine; at least, I would go there first of all."

"Let's ponder our choices tonight. So much has happened that my mind is spinning; not least because the lines which trace a route to the source of the river appear to bypass the cataracts and this would seem to suggest that we can sail the entire length unhindered, yet that would be against all my learning and study."

They slept soundly; all three curled up in the cabin of the boat as the moon rose and the stars circled above them. In the morning their minds were made to follow the map to the source of the Nile and if the map was right they would not need to abandon or carry the boat at the first cataract or any of the others.

By their reckoning in days and taking account of the stalling of the journey caused by the storm, they were twenty days out from Cairo. In ancient times it was reckoned that the journey from Swenet to Alexandria would take twenty-one to twenty-eight days. They were considerably slower but they halted every night and stopped to barter and let off the dog frequently. The proven accuracy of the map drawn on the boy's body told them that they were approaching the canal which led to Lake Moeris, the ancient man-made lake which in those times regulated the waters of the Nile via a dam and sluice.

"Are we going to the lake?" asked the boy.

"I'm not sure," answered the man, "there is a temple to be found there according to your map, beside which is drawn a minute picture of the amulet, covered with the same markings. It cannot be a coincidence; it is significant, just like the temple by the river where we found the box ..."

"We should go then."

"I am afraid for you boy. We know so little of the power as yet and I am concerned what might happen. We have not the means to defend ourselves from this ancient power if it proves to be malignant ..."

"You said it means 'PROTECTOR', so no harm will come to me, to you or to the dog ..."

"If you are sure then we will go. It is not a long journey; a little under ten miles from the junction at the river to the oasis and its waterways. The lake lies a little further on and as neither end of the canal is dammed now, we should be able to sail unimpeded."

They were in agreement and within a few hours had reached the junction which was not dammed as before. They steered the boat into the channel which was about three hundred feet wide at the widest part. The journey was uneventful and the ground either side of the canal was lush but featureless. They saw no one. It took four hours to travel the length of the canal and enter the oasis waterway system and a further hour or two to finally enter the lake.

"Where is the temple?" asked the boy.

"On the north-western side there should be perhaps the vestiges of a jetty ..."

They sailed across the lake. Scanning the bank they made out the vestiges of an ancient pier, now just a few roughhewn stones. They drew up and moored the boat. The adventurers clambered out and onto the edge of the lake.

"Was the temple near the edge of the lake?" asked the boy.

"A little distance but there should be the remains of a causeway which led to the temple from the jetty."

Scanning the terrain thereabouts, there did seem to be a path leading off into the lush margin, here at least. At its beginning it appeared as though the path might once have been edged with stones since a few remained intact.

They pushed on and within a few yards from the edge of the lake they were lost from view. The dog had scampered forward, heedless of the possibility of danger but his unbounded enthusiasm was usually a good sign and they took comfort in that. Using the odd stone which edged the path as a guide, they made their way into the dense undergrowth which still persisted. After two hundred yards, they entered a clearing; a rectangular space covered in short and rough grass which upon closer inspection seemed to be interspersed with herbs and a plant which bore tiny yellow flowers.

The man and the boy held hands as they walked and they moved forward slowly, almost gingerly, remembering the roof collapse of earlier.

"Did you bring the box?" enquired the boy.

"Yes, it is here, in my pocket," answered the man.

"Take it out," said the boy, "for if you say the map has a picture of the amulet beside the temple then I think it will help to show us the way ..."

The man took out the box, one side of which held the amulet they had found. The boy took the box from him and walked slowly into the middle of the clearing, placing the box on the ground, amulet side down and pressing down on it gently so that a good contact was made. He stepped back and returned to the man's side where they both waited. The dog joined them, a sure sign that something would soon happen; usually!

Since it was already silent, the silence gave nothing

away; not until the breeze died. Much in the same way as the map had been drawn on the young boy's body by the amulet, a fine tracery of lines started to emanate from the box. They couldn't be seen at first) but as they got thicker it was apparent that the lines were marking out the floor plan of the temple which had once stood in this space.

The box stood at its centre, marking perhaps the altar or a sacred space. Walls, openings into rooms, windows, a courtyard; all were being traced out and the lines were getting thicker all the time. The boy and the man looked closely at the lines nearest to them and it wasn't so much that the lines were being drawn but the undergrowth was moving, parting, to create the lines in the soil.

As soon as the lines were completed, a second transformation occurred. Wisps of dust heralded some movement under the ground. Silently the temple's stones grew out of the very earth and the building was raised up. Within minutes the temple had been re-erected and the white stones shone in the sunlight, blinding the amazed pair. The dog hadn't moved; he too was transfixed.

The box now rested on an altar which had grown beneath it; a stone alter, perfectly square, with the same markings as the amulet carved into each of its sides. No colour adorned the walls of the temple; it was just blank, white, luminous stone.

Man and boy had held their breath but let it out now and their breathing was the only sound which could be heard.

"What shall we do?" asked the boy.

"I don't know," replied the man, in a near whisper.

The boy let go of his hand and he approached the altar.

"Be careful!" cried out the man.

The boy stood before the altar and reached out to pick

up the box. As he did the strange luminous quality of the light around the sacred space changed and hardened, not into a beam but into a sinuous ribbon which coiled itself around the boy's arm and slowly, it wound itself around his entire body. The boy picked up the box and two things happened. The light was extinguished and the stones of the temple sank back into the ground. Once they had finally disappeared in a wisp of dust, the rough grass and the little flowering plant moved back to erase the foundations. Within a minute or two the space was as they had found it.

The boy was still standing at the centre of the space, his hand outstretched, clasping the box. He appeared to wake up and his arm fell to his side. The man was quickly by his side. The dog padded over as if nothing had happened.

The boy held out the box for the man to see. On another of its six sides there was now an amulet, bearing the same markings as the first they had found. The disc was dull though and the markings were shallow, mere scratches on the metal surface.

"Boy, how do you feel?"

"I feel both light and heavy, both dark and light and the reed in my chest has been joined by a tiny bell."

There had been another transformation; the tracery of lines which drew the map over the boy's body had also changed; some had changed colour, others appeared to show the contours of the land whilst still others had symbols and words written bedside them. The waterways were shaded a deep, sapphire blue.

"This power seeks to change you into a living map, a guide; but why?"

Studying the lines revealed that further places, temples most likely, also had the symbols beside them now. There were four marked along the course of the river, the last being at its source deep in the mountains. Each of those four places glowed like moonstones.

"Lad we must decide what to do. If each time we find one of these temples some kind of transformation takes place within you then I fear for the final outcome. It is beyond all I know and can imagine ..."

"Have no fear Father; it is a good way and the right way. We, of necessity, must visit the other four temples and allow the transformation to be completed before we visit the centre in the desert. Come, we should leave and I am tired and need to rest."

The boy took hold of the man's hand and led him back to the boat. The man was taken by the tone of the lad's voice. It had a mastery that could not be resisted and despite knowing it, he *couldn't* resist it and merely followed, the dog walking beside them, equally under its spell. At the boat the boy threw himself down and fell into a deep sleep.

The man and the dog sat on the bank, a small fire between them as they watched the sun set, the moon rise and the stars wheel overhead. In the morning the man and the dog woke to the shouts of the boy who was in the water.

Fearing that he was being attacked the man jumped up and the dog raced to the edge readying himself to plunge in for the fight. However, they were not shouts for help but shouts of joy, the source of which could not be readily comprehended. It was as if the boy was playing with a group of friends but he was alone, splashing and diving. He seemingly could not hear the man or the dog, one of which was shouting and the other barking madly.

After a time, the boy noticed them and waved, laughing all the while. The man and the dog sat back down, pondering the sight, quelling concern ... but apprehension kept surfacing; just like the boy.

The boy eventually returned to them, breathless and chattering in a strange tongue. A few minutes passed and he composed himself.

"What were you doing boy?" asked the man.

"Playing with the children; they are the spirits of the temple, ghosts of the acolytes sacrificed on the altar. They can't escape to the next place until we have accomplished our task ..."

"Did they tell you anything?"

"Many things ... We need to be wary of the temples where we will find the amulets as there are ancient curses protecting those places ..."

"Should we abandon the quest?" asked the man, his voice deep with concern.

"No, all will be well. We must be careful though and we need a few things before we attempt the next search ..."

"Things?"

"A hippopotamus's tusk and the *Unquenchable Fire* ..."

"Where ...?"

"Later Father; we must be on our way. Our journey will not remain unnoticed for much longer and the spirits can only hide our tracks until sunset. We must be back on the Nile and away from here by then. They suggest we sail tonight under the darkness of the moonless sky."

Man and dog trailed behind the boy as they made their way back to the boat where they set sail; first crossing the lake and then into the waterways of the oasis and thence to the canal and finally out into the broad river where the wind and current pushed them forward with the utmost speed.

"The spirits are with us," smiled the boy, but that was all he said.

They continued all day and all night under the moonless sky and many miles were between them and the lakeside temple by the time they rested on the dawn of the following day. The boy was quiet and insulated from them, deep in thought and mumbling in the strange tongue as before. The man busied himself with the fire and the tea. The dog, which had remained on the boat all of that time, rushed off to find relief in any number of ways and when he returned he had a less pained look!

The man and the dog rested under the shade of a tree as the sun was rising and hot. The man was worried. Things were changing and moving in ways incomprehensible to him and he felt out of his depth but the lad was confident and he did what he could. Following the lad's lead was alien to him, despite that he marvelled at the things he had already seen and the prospect of more ahead. He didn't know what the Unquenchable Fire was or where it would be found but he knew what a hippopotamus's tusk was and that could only be obtained in one way. He cleaned the gun. He'd left the comfort of his mother's and father's home to pursue a different kind of life, to find his fortune and experience something of the wonder of this Earth. Nothing so far had disappointed him. His little tasks had softened his anxiety and when the lad came-to and wandered over to get some tea, things felt less strange. The lad looked happy. The dog was dozing and kicking out his paws in his dream-bound chases.

"Are you alright Father?" asked the boy.

"Yes lad; better ... easier of mind. Still, much has happened that is strange and wonderful and it has unsettled me ..."

"Don't worry Father, all will be well ... but we must obtain the tusk soon; it will help us ..."

41

"Wrestling a tusk from a hippo will be no easy task, even with my gun. Their hides are thick and fatty and not easily pierced and they are aggressive ..."

"Perhaps we will happen upon an old or sick one and it will be less dangerous ..."

"Perchance, but we need to be wary; they could easily capsize the boat and they gather in herds ... but as I wrestled a crocodile perhaps I should be more confident in my ability ... uh?" The man laughed, remembering the incident and the boy smiled but it reminded him of a time when he felt weak and helpless.

"We will find them after the first cataract and the map says we can traverse that without carrying the boat. Soon both the map and your aim will be put to the test ..." said the boy in a voice which sounded older and wiser than it should.

"Indeed they will," replied the man, doubting his aim a lot more than the map since the map had already proved to be accurate on a number of points already.

They rested a while and then broke camp. The current was swift and the breeze stiff. To the man, it felt like the powers which dwelt here sensed their passage and approved. The boy sat on the prow of the boat and let the wind cool his body. He sensed all the landscape, both in the moment now and at a time much earlier and still the hot patch moved along the river which was drawn on his arm, moving ever closer to the cataract which they had to navigate. The map showed ancient waterways, perhaps no wider than the boat, hidden in the tangle of reeds and stones and sand levies but seemingly navigable. The first cataract was approaching but the day was drawing to an end. They hauled up and made camp.

"The sky will be clear tonight and the moon will be full," said the man.

The boy was quiet.

"Something will happen tonight Father and you must not be afraid ..."

"What my son?"

"The way will be shown to us ..."

"If you are not afraid then I shall not be either but if the way is shown then will we not have to leave?"

"Be prepared," was all the boy would say.

The man busied himself; as things became stranger he took refuge in mending things and making a box in which to stow the cube and the amulets. After sunset it became chilly and both the boy and the dog came to him and all three sat by the fire as they had done many moons ago; yet it wasn't all that many. Much had changed but the bonds between them were still strong.

It got dark and there were still a few hours before moonrise. The three had dozed by the fire but now roused themselves, the man and the dog taking their lead from the boy who appeared not agitated but expectant.

"Prepare the boat Father; it will soon be time ..."

The horizon took on a pale honey glow as the moon began her ascent. The man had prepared the boat as instructed and all three sat waiting.

"They come ..." said the boy, looking directly at the point on the horizon where the moon should appear.

At first it looked like shooting stars were raining down but as the lights got closer the man could see that they were children carrying flaming torches. The spirits from the temple began to mark the way the boat should take and it was indeed possible to navigate the cataract but without the aid of the lights there was no visible path. It was hard work for the route took many sharp turns and despite the full moon and the children's lights, everything beyond the path was strangely black; an oily black.

The man strove to keep to the way and it took all of his ken to avoid grounding the craft. Despite the chill he was sweating and breathing hard. The night went on and onwards went the boat, sometimes turning back on itself and what progress had been made seemed to be lost. As they proceeded, the lights were extinguished and if such a thing was to be any judge, they had come a fair way. The boy spoke to the children in the strange tongue he had used at the lake, thanking them for their gift of light and safe passage.

Finally the craft left the cataract behind and all the lights were gone save for the moon which suddenly blazed as if on fire before dimming to the honey gold of its rising.

"We are safe, Father. Draw in and rest."

The man navigated the craft to the shore and fair well collapsed from exhaustion.

Sneak preview of The Episode of the airship

The man slept like a log with the dog curled up in his arms. The boy didn't sleep; he sat on his haunches gazing at the moon until she set. When the sun rose and the man and the dog awoke, the boy held out his hands and taking hold of the man's with one and placing the other on the dog's head, he chanted a song, of which no words were understood by man or beast.

"Father, we must move on."

"Tell me of this *Unquenchable Fire*, lad. A hippopotamus's tusk I understand but the fire I do not; and which of them will prove to be the more dangerous to acquire?"

"The *Unquenchable Fire* is not like the fire we light to cook our food or keep ourselves warm ... it is like the fire that burns within men's hearts ... within the eyes of your enemy!"

These were strange words and none the less strange for coming from the mouth a boy.

"Where shall we find it?"

"In the valley; but we cannot walk there or sail the boat."

"I do not think we can fly."

"Have faith Father, we can and we shall fly!"

The boy fell silent and the man knew not what to think but so much of what had already happened was beyond even his wildest dreams. The boy had said that they needed to move on but which way and how?

"What do you suggest, lad?" asked the man.

"We wait for a little time. Take down the sail of the boat, Father and tie one end to the prow and the other to the bow, leaving sufficient rope to allow it to be raised above us like a cloud."

The man thought he knew what the boy meant. He took down the sail and using a length of rope he tied the top of the sail to the prow by gathering together the two corners and binding them with one end of the rope. With the other he made a slip knot and attached the rope to the prow. He did the same at the other end, attaching the rope to a cleat in the centre of the bow gunnels.

"It is done, lad; what next?"

"Watch and wait ..."

Within a few minutes the man felt a light breeze fanning his cheek. Then his ears detected a hum; a sound which was more of a flap like an untrimmed sail.

"There!" cried the boy, pointing to the south. Some distance away but not that far, a flock of birds, which appeared to be Sacred Ibis, drew closer.

The Sacred Ibis are white with black necks, legs and black plumage on their flanks. They are stately birds of a fair size. The flock neared and it began to descend. The dog became agitated. The man and the boy sat in the boat around the central mast which supported the sail like a tent above their heads. The dog hid beneath the man's knees. The birds swooped elegantly down and flew under the sail. Without missing a beat of their wings, they rose again and by some magic, the little boat rose out of the water. The man gasped and the boy smiled, knowingly and excitedly.

"We fly, Father!"

The boat rose and then turned from the south to the west. The timbers of the boat had darkened beneath the water line and with the white sail above, it resembled a huge Sacred Ibis, climbing effortlessly over the fertile margin of land beside the river towards the shimmering desert beyond.

"Where do we head for, my son?"

"The Valley of the Ibis ..."

"What are we looking for?"

"The tomb of the King. It is where we will find the *Unquenchable Fire*. Be wary, Father, the place is protected by a curse."

The dog continued to whimper. A Staffie has no head for heights, not when its nose is habitually a hair's breadth above the ground!

Rising to perhaps three hundred feet, the landscape took on the appearance of the map. A dry and dusty place dotted by green islands, traversed by paths and peppered with dark holes. The crevices were like heavy lidded eyes hewn from stone, peering out from beneath sprouting tufts of coarse grass and thorny bushes; eyes indeed; covetous and ever watchful. It was towards one of these 'dark holes' that the boat was steered. They made a very slow and gentle descent, touching down with a gentle bump. The Sacred Ibis slid out from beneath the sail and glided to an oasis some three hundred paces away.

"They will wait and return us to the river. We must wait for the sun to set and for the moon to rise. Only then will we see the guides. In daylight they appear as the angry twisting funnels of dust which drive sand into men's eyes, blinding them to the path we must follow."

"What of the tomb and the King?"

"At the tomb there will be a door which will be locked and sealed. The amulets are a key, but we cannot enter unless the King invites us in. He will ask us three questions. If we answer right he will gift us the *Unquenchable Fire*. If we answer false, we will fall prey to the curse."

"Lad, this is a dangerous undertaking and without knowing the questions, I am afraid that my strength and courage will be unequal to the task."

"Strength doesn't matter. The truth in your heart alone will be tested. The courage to try will be courage enough."

"And what of the King?"

"He is eager for us to succeed. If we succeed he will be freed."

In the three hours before sunset, the man and the boy took the dog to the oasis where they bathed and washed their clothes. They dried in the sun. When the slight coolness of the maturing afternoon made them shiver, they headed back to the boat to prepare for the test ahead.

The man loaded the gun and placed it in his belt. The gun box was home to the bag that held the wooden cube in which the amulets were set like jewels, dull, flat jewels; the one they had found in the river and the one they had received at the temple.

Two found and four still to find; the danger increasing incrementally; uncertain danger and untold riches. The man picked up the bag and tied it to his belt, squaring his shoulders and drawing in a deep breath.

"I am ready, my son; tell me what I have to do."

The boy's preparations amounted to donning his clothes and shaking his head to dispel the last few drops of water.

"We must wait for the guides. They will take us to the tomb."

"Do we take the dog?"

"I should counsel against it but I fear not even Hercules would have the strength to hold him back!"

"Have you read the stories of the Greeks?"

"They are not stories, Father ..."

The man had read the legends at his Motty's knee. The adventures which had held him in rapture then, suddenly felt like *his* labours now; minus the certainty of the strength to meet the challenge.

Made in the USA
Charleston, SC
11 June 2014